T0077544

THE LAST WIZARD

THE LAST WIZARD BEYOND MORTALS

SAMMY FAYAD

PARTRIDGE

A Penguin Random House Company

Copyright © 2014 by Sammy Fayad.

ISBN:	Hardcover	978-1-4828-2450-6
	Softcover	978-1-4828-2424-7
	eBook	978-1-4828-2425-4

All rights reserved. No part of this book may be used or reproduced by any means, graphic, electronic, or mechanical, including photocopying, recording, taping or by any information storage retrieval system without the written permission of the publisher except in the case of brief quotations embodied in critical articles and reviews.

Because of the dynamic nature of the Internet, any web addresses or links contained in this book may have changed since publication and may no longer be valid. The views expressed in this work are solely those of the author and do not necessarily reflect the views of the publisher, and the publisher hereby disclaims any responsibility for them.

To order additional copies of this book, contact
Toll Free 800 101 2657 (Singapore)
Toll Free 1 800 81 7340 (Malaysia)
orders.singapore@partridgepublishing.com

www.partridgepublishing.com/singapore

Contents

Dedication

To my friends and family, and of course, my AIS-R family.

Chapter 1

OCTOPUS AND KETCHUP

The moon smiled like a toddler, because the night was still young.

"Who are you people?" Myra Mercury asked the group of teenagers, who were led by a middle aged man.

"I'm Knox Hartley, leader of the ProDyno team of Skullcrowth." mentioned the middle aged man, expecting Myra to let him in the villa.

"Is this some kind of joke? We have no such team in Skullcrowth. Now, what do you want?" Myra asked politely.

Myra had black hair that was tied into a long ponytail, and slanted dark eyes. She was also the daughter of Sterling Gee Mercury, the mayor of Skullcrowth.

"Mayor Mercury has kindly invited all of us to dinner, so we can discuss our quest." said the man, who said his name was Knox.

"Myra! What are you doing? Let them in!" uttered the voice that came from the other end of the front hall, of the villa. It was Mayor Sterling Gee Mercury, one of the finest mayors, the dark, gothic town had ever had.

"I'm sorry, I didn't know-" Myra consoled, as she moved out of the "ProDyno" team's way. The team had five girls, and five guys, excluding Knox. The members of the ProDyno team were all around the age of 16, or 17, except Knox, of course, who had shaggy blond hair and a light beard.

Myra, who was sixteen too, waited till all the members entered the villa, and followed Knox, who was following Mayor Mercury into the dining room.

Once, all members of the ProDyno team, including Knox, were seated, Myra rushed to her bedroom to get dressed, because quite frankly she was wearing her bathrobe when she encountered the ProDyno team, at the front door of Mercury Villa.

Mercury Villa was known around town, for its ruby colored roof, and its circular driveway. It was built right after Mayor Mercury was elected, for celebration.

In her expansive bubblegum colored bedroom, Myra remembered where she had heard her father talk about the ProDynos. It was three days ago, and Myra and her father were sitting in the kitchen, eating freshly delivered shrimp rolls, from Zoe's Zeafood restaurant. Mayor Mercury had mentioned meeting with the ProDyno team, to discuss some type of quest to find a special person, or something.

Myra painted her lips a raspberry color, and then put on a single-strap dress that reached her ankles.

When Myra arrived at the dining room, the members of ProDyno stared at her like she was some kind of beauty queen. Myra sat down at the beginning of the day-long mahogany table. She sat next to a girl with strawberry blonde hair. Myra was facing Knox who was explaining something to Mayor Mercury, who was at the head of the table.

There was octopus tentacles on the big silver-plate that was placed on the middle of the table. Myra had wanted to call the maid to serve the ProDynos, but then she realized that they had already served themselves. Each member had a glass of diet Coke, next to his or her big plate of octopus tentacles.

"Excuse me," said one of the members, to the maid who passed by his seat, "do you have any ketchup? This octopus is way too dry."

Chapter 2

THE QUEST

Myra listened closely to her father's conversation with Knox, as she sucked on the octopus tentacle, the maid put on her plate.

"So, you're telling me you want me to take them all to the north, to check if he's still there?" Knox gulped.

"He might still be there, the last wizard on earth; do you know what we could do with his magic? Skullcrowth, it has been dark and scary looking forever, that is why we have no tourists, no nothing. If we can find him, and get the magic, we can make Skullcrowth a better place." raged the mayor, with wisdom.

"Daddy, sorry to interrupt but how can magic make Skullcrowth a better place, you think it is just a spell, or a swing of a wand, impossible." Myra tuned in. Knox and Mayor Mercury turned to Myra.

"Sweetie, it is impossible, these days, yes. But, with actual magic, you could do anything." Mayor Mercury emitted.

"He has a point," mentioned the strawberry blonde girl who sat next to Myra. "I'm Buttercup."

"Myra." Myra smiled back at the girl, who surprisingly looked very similar to her in a weird way, other than the hair and the eyes, of course.

"Why are you guys risking your lives for this?" Myra asked Buttercup.

"Skill and strength runs in the family, so I joined the ProDyno team, an ultimate experience, for free. It trains you how to survive in harsh climates and fight against the evil. Plus, if we do something that helps the government, like we are going to do now, we get paid." Buttercup explained.

"Cool, real cool," Myra answered. She thought about what it would be like to be in such a team. "Daddy, can I talk to you?"

"Sure." Mayor Mercury headed out of the dining room with his daughter, and then they went to the chic modern kitchen.

"Daddy, I like it, this team..." Myra started but got interrupted.

"DON'T EVEN THINK ABOUT IT, YOUNG LADY. I AM SURE YOUR MOTHER WHO IS IN A BETTER PLACE, RIGHT NOW, WOULD NOT LIKE IT IF YOU DROPPED OUT OF SCHOOL TO JOIN SOME TEAM THAT WORKS FOR THE GOVERMENT." roared the mayor, as he marched out of the kitchen. A few seconds later, Knox appeared at the doorway.

"May I ask where the bathroom is?" Knox questioned.

"Mr. Hartley, I talked with my dad and he allows me to join the ProDyno team." lied Myra eagerly, out of the blue.

"Ms. Mercury, joining the team requires experience, strength, skill, and I doubt that Mayor Mercury would allow his little princess to join such a team on a harsh quest." answered Knox.

"He did allow it, and, I could learn everything the team knows." Myra pointed out.

"The only way you could join the team, at the moment, is if we lose a member, or if we are desperate. And none of that is happened, or is going to happen. Now, please tell me where the bathroom is." sighed Knox.

"Across the hall, then take a right." Myra empathized. Knox thanked her and then left.

Myra was furious, she always got what she wanted, and she was going to make sure she did. And then, an idea popped in her head. Myra went back to the dining room, and said she wanted to go to bed, said goodbye, and then zoomed upstairs and locked her bedroom door, behind her.

She stripped off her dress, and then put on ripped grey jeans, a black shirt, black boots (with heels), and tucked her black hair into a black cap, that she also put on. Myra then wiped off the lipstick and makeup she put on, and then slipped her smart phone in her jeans pocket. After that, she ripped off a piece of paper from her math notebook, which was lying on her desk. She jotted a few words onto the paper and then placed it on her bed. Finally, Myra took the covers off the second bed, that was in her room (if friends slept over) and tied the covers around a leg that held up her bed. Myra pushed her window open, and threw the attached cover outside; she watched as the covers tangled down the villa exterior, and landed on the grass, gently. Then, she threw a stack of money into her small black purse, and threw the purse out the window as she held onto the covers and got out of the window, making her way from the second, to the first floor exterior.

Myra left the cover hanging, and then ducked under every window she needed to pass, grasping onto her purse. Then, she peered to the front of the villa, and waited till she saw the ProDyno team divide into two groups, each group getting into a dark grey van. Myra walked silently from tree to tree, till she reached a black Jaguar xk120. She yanked open the car door, got into the driver's seat, started the car, and then followed silently behind.

Chapter 3

SOUL SWITCHERS

Myra watched from her roofless Jaguar xk120, as one of the vans made a stop next to a small farmhouse that was next to a fast food restaurant. A girl with strawberry blonde hair got out and waved at the van as it sped out of the area. It was Buttercup. Myra got out of the car, locked it, and then rushed after Buttercup, who was searching for keys to open the front door of the farmhouse. Myra fished a pistol out of her pocket (that she stole from the Mercury Villa guard, as she sneaked out after the two vans) and placed it against the side of Buttercup's head.

"Don't scream, shout, yell, cry, or beg. Just open the door without looking back, and get in." Myra whispered into Buttercup's ear.

Back in the Mercury Villa, Mayor Mercury went upstairs to check on his only daughter. He was just about to turn the knob...

"Sir, you have a phone call," said the maid.

✶✶✶✶

Myra learned that Buttercup lived alone, Myra and Buttercup were sitting on the same couch; Buttercup answering different questions while Myra pointed a pistol at her.

"Look, you're asking for too much, I can't accept it. I didn't know you were this eager and self-absorbed." shuddered Buttercup.

"Do you really think it's smart to insult someone who is pointing a gun at you?" Myra scowled.

"Fine, I'll do it," Buttercup retorted. "Tomorrow we will go and trade looks, and then I'll go back to your place and see what it's like to live like a princess."

"No. We are going now, I have limited time and if my dad finds out that I ran away, he'll lock me in my room forever. I put a note that explains everything just in case he finds out, early," sighed Myra, "now, get up."

Once Myra and Buttercup were in the Jaguar xk120, Myra pointed the gun at Buttercup while she let her drive. The streets of Skullcrowth were dim of lights and empty of people.

When they reached the beauty salon, they got in, and then got out an hour later, looking completely different. Myra had long strawberry blonde hair, the tips left black (because Myra never liked light hair without having some dark in it). And, Buttercup had frizzy black hair and black extensions, because her real hair wasn't as long as the actual Myra's. Also, slight changes were showered onto both of their faces, because obviously they weren't twins, to look the same.

When they reached back at the farmhouse, they traded clothes and then sat down to discuss everything else.

"Look, I'm sure my dad didn't notice my disappearance yet, because there is no police driving around town, yet, but you have exactly half an hour to get there. Don't wake up the guards, and don't put on the headlights of the car. Plus, get in from the window, not the front door. Lastly, my dad thinks I'm asleep, so go to sleep directly, but unlock my bedroom door." the words flew out of Myra's mouth.

"How am I supposed get in by the window? Isn't your bedroom window on the second floor?" wearied Buttercup.

"Yes, but you'll figure out which window and how once you get there. Here, take," said Myra as she gave her shiny black purse to Buttercup, "there is money and my car key in here, plus some makeup. Anymore questions?"

"Nope, but you need to know a few things before I go. I am dating Trent, which means you are dating Trent. And, I'm not a big fan of Gwyneth, which means you aren't a big fan of Gwyneth. Got it?" said Buttercup.

"Then who are my friends?"

"Caprice, Alexia, and Preston."

"Okay..." Myra followed herself (Buttercup) to the door, and watched herself getting into her black Jaguar xk120, and then watched the roofless car flash out of the area.

All Myra had left, was her smart phone and her pistol. Myra looked around the farmhouse, it was small, containing; two bedrooms, two bathrooms, a kitchen, a sitting room, and a basement. Everything in the farmhouse was normal and cheap, but when Myra went downstairs to the basement, it was like another planet.

Chapter 4

Not Reality

Governor Mercury finally finished his phone call and went back to Myra's bedroom, to check on her. He turned the knob, the door opened, and "Myra" was lying on her bed, sound asleep.

It was still night, precisely 11:00 PM. And the real Myra was fooling around in the farmhouse's basement, which was filled with millions of weapons, from; bow & arrows, to machine guns, to knives and swords. Myra grabbed a katana and pretended she was having a duel. Then, her tummy rumbled, so she ran upstairs to the kitchen, and looked around. She never had to make anything by herself, because they had a maid. But now, she had no choice but to make *something* for herself. So, she took a jar of peanut butter out of the old rusty fridge, and placed it on the little dining table, that took half the kitchen's space. In ten minutes, Myra was nibbling on the worst sandwich she had ever tasted in her entire life.

At 7:30 AM the next morning, there was a knock at the farmhouse's front door. Myra was lying on the master bedroom bed, a king sized rusty bed, when she heard the knock. She picked up the katana she was playing with the night before, and headed to the front door. Then, Myra peeked through the sidelight of the wooden door. On the front porch, stood an average sized, light brown haired boy, probably sixteen or seventeen years old. He looked fit and had broad shoulders. Myra realized that he was a member of the ProDyno team; she saw him the night before, at the Mercury Villa.

Myra had slept with the clothes she wore the day before, Buttercup's trade clothes. So, she ran to the master bedroom, changed the smelly clothes she was wearing immediately, and then brushed her teeth in the master bathroom. Finally, she opened the front door, and the guy was still standing there, he wore; a steel armor (from shoulder to toe), and a long sword was attached to his hip.

"What took you so long?" the boy said, then wrapped his arms around Myra and kissed her on her rosy lips. Myra usually would've slapped him, but she had to play along, and, she weirdly liked it. They stood there for a minute, lips meeting, but they stopped when they heard an ear ripping noise. Myra didn't notice the van in the background, it was a ProDyno van.

"Why aren't you wearing your armor, Buttercup?" asked the boy as he backed away from her.

"I forgot... um... where I put them," mentioned Myra nervously.

"They should be downstairs." the guy walked past her and trotted downstairs, to the weapon-full basement. In seconds, he came rushing back up, with; an upper body armor (made of steel), a lower body armor (made of steel), and a helmet (made of steel).

"I have to wear that?!" Myra gulped, as she went to the master bedroom to get her katana.

"Safety, babe. Now, help me fill this bag with weapons." the guy grabbed a duffle bag that was placed on the porch, and went back downstairs. Myra followed after she grabbed her katana.

In ten minutes, time, Myra looked like a female knight, as she and her "boyfriend" took a heavy bag of weapons to the dark grey van. A girl with platinum blonde hair popped into view, when the van back seat doors opened.

"BUTTERCUP! WHAT TOOK YOU SO LONG! TRENT JUST STOOD THERE FOR AN HOUR, WAITING FOR YOU!" roared the platinum blonde haired girl, who also looked like a female knight. Anyways, Myra had just remembered, his name was Trent. The real Buttercup had told her the night before.

"Caprice, calm down," Trent got in the van, and sat next to a guy with black hair reaching his brows, and grey eyes that reminded Myra of a storm.

"Come on, you know I hate waiting!" whined the blonde girl, Caprice.

Myra jumped into the van, and noticed that everyone in the van was wearing armor, too. PHEW, she passed Caprice, Trent, and the grey eyed dude, then took a seat next to a girl with auburn hair combed to one side, behind Trent and his friend.

The front of the van, where the driver was, was separated from the back seats of the van, by a velvet curtain. The back part of the van, had leather seats that were put like a bus, two on the right side, two on the left side, and the same applied to the row behind. The van was only half as big as a normal bus, so it only fit eight people, nine, if you count the driver. Myra wondered why the ProDyno team would bring a bus, instead, because it would fit all of them.

"Since when did you ever sit next to me?" asked the girl with auburn hair.

"There isn't any other place to sit." Myra pointed out.

"Oh, yeah,"

In the front row of the van, sat; Trent and the grey eyed dude, on one side, and, Caprice and a girl with dark skin and black hair, on the other. On the last/second row, sat; Myra and the auburn haired girl, on one side, and two guys on the other side. One of the guys had tan skin and spiky blond hair, while the other had dark skin and a buzz-cut.

"Where are the others?" Myra said when she realized that there were three people missing, from the eleven. The van had already started moving, and was already out the area, and speeding on a highway.

"Ruby, Mr. Hartley, and Preston went to get some food. Mr. Hartley decided that we didn't need the other van, for the quest, so we're all, as you can see, are squished in here." answered the auburn haired girl. "What happened, to your hair?"

"Um... I wanted to try black, so I dip dyed and added extensions," Myra remembered.

"Nice. Ukkhh, we'll reach Mount Upaithric in hours. Ruby, Preston, and Mr. Hartley are going to follow us." sighed the girl.

"Buttercup, why are you sitting next to her?" Caprice said coldly from the first row of the van.

"I'm not called *her*, I'm called GWYNETH." barked auburn haired Gwyneth.

"Your name is so stupid, please don't tell me your actual parents called you that?" giggled the dark skinned girl, next to fair Caprice.

"Alexia? I mean who on earth would think about such a name, that sounds like bird poop!" roared Gwyneth.

"Shut it! STOP, no more unnecessary drama!" Trent called from the front seat.

"Fine, what evs'," dark skinned Alexia and fair skinned Caprice, said in the same time.

Myra was feeling like a retard, at that moment, she remembered Buttercup telling her to not LIKE Gwyneth, and to LIKE Caprice and Alexia.

Back in Skullcrowth, in the Mercury Villa, the real Buttercup sat on the edge of a bed, thinking. It was Myra's bedroom, so girly and expensive looking.

Buttercup had lost her parents, ages ago, so she was stuck with an older brother who spent his days mopping the floors of a downtown club, and sleeping with a prostitute, in her tiny apartment. Buttercup sighed, then slipped the stack of money (Myra gave her) into her jeans pocket and marched downstairs, to the sitting room, where Myra's father was sitting.

"Good morning, daddy!" Buttercup said trying to sound exactly like Myra.

"Sweetie, are you going out to the mall, today? Ultranne called," mentioned Mayor Mercury.

"Ultranne? Oh...yeah...sure." Buttercup replied.

"She's coming to pick you up in an hour. Your credit card, debit card, and wallet are full. Enjoy!" Mayor Mercury smiled.

"Debbaaa debbaa... debit... card?" Buttercup whispered in shock. She knew that Myra was rich, and was treated like a princess, but she didn't know Myra got everything. "Thank you, DADDY!!!"

Chapter 5

RICH AND POOR

It was 2:00 PM. Ultranne, a pink haired millionaire had picked Buttercup up, with her Mercedes Benz sports car, hours before. At the moment, they were at Quartzite Plaza, the mall with the most expensive shops in the city. Unlike Buttercup, who was wearing normal-casual clothes, Ultranne was wearing; diamond earrings, red high heel shoes, a sparkly blouse, and red tights. Plus, Ultranne's pink hair was combed and ear length, while Buttercup's long black hair was all over the place and not brushed.

"So? Speak!" mumbled Ultranne as she and Buttercup sat on a bench, in the mall.

"I need a new phone," Buttercup replied, with a quick excuse.

"Apple store it is. Come on," The two rich sixteen year olds got up, and headed to the Apple store.

"Excuse me? One iPhone please, gold colored with rhinestones stuck to the back," Ultranne demanded as they approached the salesman.

"Oh, so from the bling section, am I right?" asked the skinny salesman, who led the two girls to an open doorway, next to the cashier's desk.

"In here, our lowest prices are $500. Please see if there is anything that interests you, ladies, there is more than rhinestones and gold in here."

Beyond the doorway was a dim room filled with display cases. The display cases each had both a fancy tablet and a phone. But, they weren't just any phones or tablets; there were some that were gold colored, some that had diamonds stuck to the back, and some that had rhinestones *and* diamonds stuck to the back.

Buttercup walked to one display case; it had a gold colored iPhone and a white tablet with diamonds stuck to the back. There was a price tag curled around the display case's handle. On the price tag, was the number; *$2800*.

"Two thousand eight hundred dollars?! That is A LOT!" Buttercup yelped, but then remembered her "father" was rich, and the governor. "Joking, I could buy a hundred of these, hahaha."

"I know, right?!" Ultranne agreed.

"So? Do you want to buy this case?" asked the salesman.

"Yes, sure," Buttercup grinned to the salesman, "I'll pay cash."

The beautiful painting of sky was getting darker, from the ProDyno van-window, point of view- and not just because the windows were tinted. Myra noticed their surroundings were changing and the climate was getting a lot colder. Ice started to sprout out of nowhere, after the van passed a wooden sign, planted on the road, which said; *Mount Upaithric*.

"Hello...yeah...I think...sure...where...okay...bye." said Trent as he flipped his phone shut, ending his call with Mr. Hartley. He was still sitting next to the grey eyed guy, named Xavier. Myra had noticed that not just Trent was fit and sportive like, but all the ProDyno team was fit, especially Ethan and Dylan. Ethan was the guy with blond hair spiking out of his head, and Dylan was the dude with the buzz-cut and dark skin. They both sat in the two seats on the left side of the second row of seats, in the van.

"What did he say?" asked Alexia.

"He said that he is waiting for us, with Ruby and Preston, at a place called Zoe's Zeafood?" answered Trent. Myra's heart sank, when Trent said the restaurant name. She remembered when she and her father ordered from Zoe's Zeafood. They had loved the food and enjoyed their day. Sterling Gee Mercury was a good mayor, but an extraordinary father; Myra wanted to burst into tears thinking about him, but stayed strong.

"Tell me when we reach," yawned Gwyneth as she went back to her heavy sleeping and snoring.

"I want to take this off so badly!" uttered Myra when the van halted to a complete stop, minutes later in a snow covered wooden restaurant. "And by **that** I mean the armor."

"Just watch me." Ethan smirked as everyone stood up, and then pulled on his upper body armor. The full armor came off easily, revealing a long sleeved shirt and jeans. "See, easy. By the way, I know you aren't Buttercup."

"Haha. What? You are so funny!" giggled Myra. "Of course I'm Buttercup, if I wasn't do you think I would do this?"

Myra grabbed her katana that she carried around, since her first step out of the farmhouse, and sliced through the leather seat she was just sitting on. The upper part of the leather seat flopped to the ground.

"News flash, Buttercup would never do that, now, who are you?" Dylan questioned as he and everyone else on the van took off their armor, in the same way Ethan did.

"I'm Myra Mercury, daughter of Governor Mercury, who kindly invited you guys to dinner, for this quest I don't really get," sighed Myra as she took off her armor, too. "I would take off my wig, to show you my real hair, but, this isn't a wig."

"I knew it, Buttercup never-ever-ever would like Gwyneth," laughed Caprice.

"Please, please, please don't tell Mr. Hartley!" Myra begged.

"What's funny is that I like you way more than the actual Buttercup, so why not? I promise, not to tell." said Ethan.

"Hey, watch it," Trent's eyebrows lowered. "I knew our kiss was too good to be true, Myra. Where is my Buttercup?!"

"We made a deal, and she is in good hands. In fact your girlfriend is probably spending thousands of dollars from my wallet right now." barked Myra. "Now, promise you won't tell, or else."

"Or else what?" Trent frowned. "You can't possibly do..."

"I could tell my dad that I'm here, so, he would find out that Buttercup is a fake and plus torture her until she says where I am, and with who." Myra interrupted.

"Like father, like daughter, evil!" said Caprice disgustedly. "I'm sure you could never convince me, not to tell."

"Want a bet?" asked Myra as she slipped out a pair of diamond earrings from her pocket, and handed it to Caprice. "Now do you promise?"

"Want to be BFF's?" grinned Caprice as she snatched the shiny earrings from Myra's palm.

"Sorry, I think I already have one, and so do you." Myra pointed out. "Gwyneth, you are the most down-to-earth person I've ever met!"

"Aww, of course I won't tell, Myra," Gwyneth hugged Myra with a friendly smile.

"Now, what do you guys want?" Myra questioned Xavier, Alexia, and Dylan. Alexia asked for Myra's gold plated silver bracelet, Dylan said they were cool, and Xavier just promised he wouldn't open his mouth.

"Since all of you traitors are convinced, let us get a move on, we're late." Trent puffed as he got out of the van, wearing casual clothes and leaving his armor behind.

Chapter 6

THE MEETING

Knox Hartley was sitting at a booth, with a dark haired girl and a silver haired guy. Gwyneth had told Myra earlier that Mr. Hartley was with "Ruby" and "Preston", so obviously you could tell who the dude was, and who the dudette was.

Zoe's Zeafood was quite impressive, especially since there was more than one in the country. The restaurant reminded Myra of home, because the Zoe's Zeafood restaurant, next to the Mercury Villa was exactly the same, except the one she was in now was in a cold climate.

"Ruby!" Gwyneth said in excitement, as she rushed to the dark haired girl that stood up from her seat to return Gwyneth's hug.

"Preston!" Caprice and Alexia smiled at the silver haired dude.

"Mr. Hartley, glad to see you again." Trent shook hands with the tired looking Mr. Hartley, who had shaved his light beard and got a haircut.

"Oh I remember this place! I love the squid here!" Xavier lilted, moving his black hair away from his grey eyes. They were finally, all sitting in a bigger table, no longer a booth. And, Myra had ordered the shrimp rolls, to remind her of home, while, Gwyneth and Ruby, talked and talked, and talked.

"Where do they get all this seafood anyways? We had octopus in the governor's house, and now I'm having the best eel." Ruby questioned as she sliced a piece of cooked eel, in half.

"Bliquerdorf Sea, duh!" acknowledged Caprice, who slightly looked better than Ruby, who had perfect features.

"So, Trent, Butter, how is..." Ruby said with a giggle.

"We broke up." interrupted Trent, with a frown.

"Buttercup Quinn Archerson! Why the hell didn't you tell me?!" demanded the silver haired Preston, with his demanding black eyes.

"Oh, about the breakup? It's not... important." Myra got up from her place, grabbed a jug of lemonade and poured it over Trent's head. "Because I feel way better, now."

"Preston, they didn't even tell us, so don't act surprised." mentioned Alexia; her hands covered her mouth, so the laughter wouldn't be heard. The sight of Trent getting soaked with lemonade was quite hysterical, especially for a naive girl, like Alexia.

"Oh, I don't care. I was asking about the weird dip dye." Preston laughed.

"HAHAHAHAHAHAHAHAHAHAHAHAHA! I guess you are free now, Trent!" Caprice grabbed the soaked Trent by the hand, and led him to the restaurant bathrooms.

"Serves him right." Myra grinned, as she went back to her seat.

"Um... ma'am, your shrimp rolls?" the waiter placed a plate of rolls on the table, and then dashed back into the kitchen.

"Smells delightful, Buttercup. May I have a word with you?" Mr. Hartley looked at the mouthwatering rolls, with the mouthwatering smell.

"No need, for a word, I have a confession to make," Myra flipped her dyed strawberry blonde hair. "I'm not Buttercup; I'm Myra, Myra Mercury."

Chapter 7

$REST IN PEACE$

"You mindless child!" thundered Mayor Mercury at his only daughter. "You spent more than your allowance! How could you waste so much!"

"Mayor Mercury, I'm Buttercup Archerson, pleased to meet you!" Buttercup said, as she stood at the doorway of the Mercury Villa, with shopping bags in her grasp. "Nope, not really. I bought a ticket to Paradise Islands, an amazing iPhone, a tablet, designer clothes, perfume, a small apartment, and a pair of new shoes. Only, thanks for the money, Daddy."

Mayor Mercury just stared at the girl, real hard. She spoke the truth, she wasn't Myra. "Where is my daughter?! And what did you do to her?!"

Buttercup explained everything, and then the mayor pulled out his phone, and made a phone call.

"Hello?" shouted Mayor Mercury onto the phone.

"Yes," answered a familiar voice.

"Listen, you bastard, how dare you take my daughter without my permission?!" yelled the mayor.

"Mayor Mercury, I was expecting your call. There is no way I would take Myra without your permission, in fact, I didn't know she was Myra until she blurted it out." mentioned Knox Hartley. "If you haven't noticed, she disguised herself as our fellow teammate, Buttercup."

"I don't care if she disguised as a pig! Send her back, or else, you will lose your job and lose Buttercup." scolded Mayor Mercury as he hung up.

"Buttercup? Is it?" the mayor examined Buttercup.

"Yes, sir," answered Buttercup.

"Listen, girly, I had a good impression on everyone. That is why I got elected, but, my weakness is my daughter, and you are not stepping out of this house, until she comes back." frowned Mayor Mercury. "Ernest! Take her to the basement, and lock her in the blue bedroom."

A bulky giant walked to the confused Buttercup, and dragged her downstairs. "YOU CAN'T D..."

Myra Mercury studied Knox. He looked stressed and depressed. They were heading to Knox's red Chevrolet Corvette, leaving everyone else in the group to go in the van.

"Listen, Myra. It is my only choice. I am taking you back, to where you belong," sighed Knox Hartley as he started the red sports car, once both of them were in.

"Wait, we could work this out." Myra pulled out a stack of a hundred dollar bills, from a duffel bag. "My dad doesn't know yet. Here,"

"I'm afraid, he does know. He called me. Buttercup is in danger, unless you go back." Knox Hartley muttered, taking a long stare at the stack of money. "But, who cares about Buttercup. We can work this out."

Myra put on a guilty smile, as Knox snatched the money from her clenched hand, and controlled the car out the Zoe's Zeafood parking lot.

Buttercup Archerson lay on an uncomfortable bed, in a windowless bedroom, in Mercury Villa. The bedroom was cramped, and only contained a single bed, a dresser, and book shelves, along with an on-suite windowless bathroom.

Buttercup wiped a flood of tears from her face, and then tried the knob on the wooden double doors, hoping the triple lock would break into millions of pieces.

"Hahahahahahahahahahaha!" the bulky man that brought her to the room laughed. He had stood in the room stalking Buttercup. Ernest was his name, but his name's meaning had nothing to do with his actual personality.

"What are you going to do?! Rape me?" fumed Buttercup at the giant.

The man stopped laughing, then kneeled down and pulled out a long whip from under the bed.

****

A red sports car halted to a complete stop, two feet away from Bliquerdorf Sea. The sea was coated with silver ice, which sparkled more than Caprice Carter's sparkling coat.

The ProDyno group was waiting for their leader, and their unexpected new member, for minutes. The grey ProDyno van had left the area because obviously the driver had nothing to do with the quest.

"What took you so long? Myra?" Caprice snapped.

"Let's get a move on!" insisted Knox as he put on his armor, and told everyone else to, too. "The ice is strong enough to walk on, trust me."

Alexia rolled her eyes and walked onto the ice. "Duh!"

Then a crack broke through the silver surface. And, the ground below Alexia collapsed. Alexia's thin body slipped into the freezing water, but, she never came back up again.

"Alex!" Caprice cried, running to the hole, but Preston stopped her at her place. "Let me go!"

Knox stared at the hole, expecting Alexia's black hair to fly up. But there was no sign of her.

"We're just going to leave her?" asked Dylan, with an elegant English accent.

"I can't let anyone take another risk, rest in peace, or pieces, Alex." uttered Knox with a dull tone. "It is too dangerous."

"Then how are we going to cross to the mountain?" questioned Xavier with his storm-grey eyes.

"The girl is probably drowning down there! And you're thinking of how to get to the other side?!" demanded Preston. He walked to Xavier and stuck a dagger into his leg. "B****!"

Xavier sunk down to his knees with pain, while Dylan, Ethan, and Trent pushed angry Preston away. Caprice ignored the fight and kneeled down, to put her fair hand in the water, hoping to find a body. Knox, Ruby, Myra and Gwyneth just stood there, consuming all the drama.

"Gwen, get in the car. Mr. Hartley, we'll try to find a way to the other side." Myra informed the leader, and then got into the cadmium red car with Gwyneth.

By the time Myra and Gwyneth got back from the useless road trip, there was still no sign of Alexia, and all the team members were filled with hatred and anger.

"Guys, our only option, is this." said Knox as he took off his armor and told everyone else to, too. He got into his car, started it, and went backwards, then sped to the frozen sea's direction. Right before falling into the icy sea, the car door opened and Knox jumped out. The sports car crashed into the ice, breaking it into pieces and causing the car to float in one place. The car was ten feet away from the edge of the hard ground, where the jaw-dropped team members stood.

"We'll meet on the top of... my... baby," Knox's face was planted with bloody scars from the jump. He got up and then dived into the negative temperature-d water.

"I'll help." insisted Trent to his injured teammate. Xavier nodded with pain, and then was dragged into the water. The rest of the team un-delightfully followed into the harsh water. Trent struggled while helping Xavier across the water, but not as much as Caprice, who had just lost her best friend and ruined her leather boots.

Chapter 8

PLAIN PAIN

"STOP, PLEASE!" Buttercup Archerson yelled in pain, as Ernest the giant slashed her topless back with a whip, for the twenty fifth time. "PLEASE!"

"Not until we reach Mayor Mercury's age," Ernest slashed the whip again, "twenty six."

The wooden double doors' lock, unlocked, and in came the fumed mayor. "Enough."

"But, sir, I-" Ernest said, but got interrupted.

"I said ENOUGH. Put her shirt back on. Listen, Buttercup, if my daughter doesn't return by tomorrow, you are coming with me to search for her." said the mayor, he left the room and triple locked it again.

"Get, off, me." Buttercup shouted at the giant. The giant put the whip under the single blue bed, and then rested on an expensive armchair, that the mayor put in as Ernest's bed.

Hours later, Ernest's snores filled the bedroom. Buttercup stared with disgust, and then headed to the on-suite bathroom, searching for a weapon. She found toothpaste, a toothbrush, shaving cream, a plunger, lotion, a jug, combs, face wash, towels, and a hair dryer. Buttercups poured shaving cream, lotion, face wash and toothpaste into the jug, and then mixed them together with the toothbrush, making it plainly disgusting. Then, Buttercup placed the jug on the floor, next to the snoring giant, and went back to the bathroom to fetch the hair dryer, a comb, a towel, and the plunger.

With the filled jug in one hand, and a comb in the other, Buttercup was ready. She spilled the mixture in the jug over the sleeping giant's head. Then, as Ernest awoke, Buttercup brushed his wet hair with a comb.

"What are you doing?!" Ernest yelled.

Buttercup dropped the comb, then picked up the plunger and stuck it on Ernest's big nose. Finally, Buttercup hair-dried the giant with the hair dryer and strangled him with a towel, till he lost breath.

"Just a breath taking makeover." grinned Buttercup, as she tied the passed-out giant's body parts around the armchair, using towels. "Now, where is that whip?"

****

There was a breeze that slowed the boat, or to be exact, the red-car-boat-that-didn't-sink-yet. Ethan, Trent, and Dylan were pushing the half-sunken car along the water, because there were no paddles. While the rest of the team sat on the car roof, keeping Ethan, Trent, and Dylan updated with the direction of the car.

Myra, Ruby, and Preston were on the car hood, for some privacy and more space.

"Stupid ***** a** Xavier" moaned Preston, looking disgustedly at poor Xavier who was talking with Gwyneth, on the car roof.

"Calm down, Prissy, you stuck a knife in his leg!" Ruby rolled her eyes, her dark hair shined in the sunlight. Even though, the sun was about to set, soon, any sunlight helped.

"Everyone, get comfortable, your beds are the places you're sitting on, right now. Please put your hands together for our paddlers who are, hopefully, going to make sure we don't sink when we are asleep." sighed middle aged Knox Hartley.

Myra wasn't too happy about where she was going to sleep, but, she was tired after that long day: awaken at seven thirty, Alexia's death (possibly dead), memories of her dad, and so on.

"I am not risking my life. I am not going to sleep here!" barked Caprice from the car roof. "I don't care! You have to find another place."

"Look, we're getting closer to the mountains!" Ruby mentioned with delight.

"We can probably reach there in thirty minutes, Preston, go help them." said Knox, with wrinkles under his eyes.

"Oh, I'm going, but, why doesn't that lazy bum over there do it too?" scolded Preston, while looking at Xavier.

"Why don't you understand, you knifed my f****** leg!" Xavier jumped from the car roof, to the car hood (where Preston was standing) and pushed Preston off the car, and into the arctic water. Then, Preston climbed back onto the car hood, and threw a punch, but Xavier blocked it, and smashed his fist into Preston's nose, which caused Preston to fall back into the chilly water.

"Stop!" Caprice yelled at Xavier. She charged down at Xavier, halberd in hand, and sliced Xavier's ankle off.

"Ukhh!" Xavier puffed; he no longer had a left foot, just blood spilling down his sliced ankle. He fell backward, bumping his head on a tiny iceberg floating in the water. The team watched in horror, as Xavier floated on his back, along the sea.

"Why the hell would you do that?!" Myra asked with anger.

"I lost Alex, I'm not going to lose Prissy." snapped Caprice with guilt. Ethan, Trent, and Dylan were sent to Xavier's aid. But, they didn't realize the swarming sharks ahead of the floating car. The three directly took unconscious Xavier back to the car-boat, but, Preston was still floating in the water, near the huge sharks. In seconds, a shark's open mouth gulped down the screaming Preston, and then rushed back to its shark group. Caprice's eyes fired at the footless Xavier, whose head was bursting with blood.

"It's your entire fault, all your fault!" Caprice shed a tear, wishing Preston was still alive.

"I know, I feel guilty, but this is life." said Knox cheerfully. "I'm sure Xavier didn't want Preston do get gulped down, by a shark!"

"He should be... alright," approved Ethan, "but we can't push the car anymore, and it's going to sink."

"Alright?! That doesn't look alright to me." frowned Ruby, placing Xavier's bloody head, on her lap and wrapping it with plaster that she ripped from the car-boat's interior.

"Alright?! You're talking about the guy who caused Prissy's death?! Ukkhh you are heartless dopes." Caprice hugged herself tightly, because it didn't look like anyone else even cared.

Chapter 9

GROUNDED

"What? Happened, here?" sighed Mayor Mercury. "Get him out of that!"

"Mayor Mercury, please let me go, please! I don't know where they are, I promise." begged Buttercup. The mayor was tired and didn't have time to feel sorry for a little peasant girl, so he pushed her out of his way and started helping the passed-out-Ernest.

When Ernest was back to his giant-self, he gave Buttercup a few whips and then left the bedroom to help the mayor and his security, search for Myra and the ProDyno team.

Buttercup Archerson stared at herself in the small ancient mirror, which was above the sink, in the on-suite bathroom of the basement bedroom.

"Who am I?" Buttercup whispered, staring at her long fake Myra-like black hair, that was messy and flopping around. Then Buttercup remembered the time she had with Ultranne; buying, buying, and buying. It was quite fun to feel rich, then.

The sports car was beginning to sink, but fortunately the ProDyno team was getting close to land.

"FINALLY!" Caprice jumped off the floating vehicle and landed perfectly on hard ice land. The floating vehicle floated next to a tall and wide mountain, covered in white crystals.

Once every member was on land, they started hiking upward.

"He lives on the top of this isolated hill." Knox pointed out.

"By **he** you mean the wizard?" asked Gwyneth with reddish eyes.

"What do you think?" snapped Xavier, hopping on his good leg.

"Do we put our armor on, now? Sir?" Dylan questioned.

"Armor? HAHAHAHAHAHAHAHA, NO. Instead… Watch and learn," Knox pulled out a tiny machine with a button on it, and pressed it. Leather body armor with white fur grew on each of the members of the team. It covered their full body except for their heads, but it fit in comfortably since the leather kept them comfortable and the fur made them warm.

"I love these boots!" Ruby rejoiced as she bent down to look at the cowhide boots with fur puffing on the top that covered her casual sneakers.

"Everyone, take out your weapons, there is a pack of wolves in the distance. I'm going to check if my baby sunk yet." said Knox sadly.

Myra used a bow & arrow, Caprice used a mace, Trent used a falchion, Gwyneth used a katar dagger, Ethan used a war-hammer, Ruby used a sickle, Xavier used a halberd, and when Knox came, he used a hunting shotgun. The Arctic wolves who had snow-white fur attacked the members of the ProDyno team, one wolf almost jumped on Ethan, but Myra aimed with her bow & arrow and knocked off the wolf, which was an inch away from Ethan.

"Thanks!" Ethan said as he slammed another wolf's head, with his war-hammer. Back to back, Ruby thrashed a huge wolf's neck off with her sickle, and Gwyneth stabbed her katar dagger into another wolf's rear end. Panicking, Xavier was on the icy floor getting bitten at by an Arctic wolf with darker-white fur, but Trent noticed and sliced his falchion through the wolf's body.

Knox on the other hand, stood in the distance like Myra and shot at as much wolves as possible, while Caprice banged her mace into two wolves at a time, very closely.

"Oh shit! It looks like there is a storm coming!" Knox examined the weather with a gulp. It was past sunset and it was pretty dark, but the heavy winds and large snow dropping from the sky was an obvious storm-starter. "Quick! Take out the wolves and then follow me."

Once the team got their last bruises from the Arctic wolves, they killed them and followed Knox uphill. Knox kept on going until the storm got worse, and until they actually found a little cave, which was under a little slope hill.

"Everyone, I'm really sorry for almost letting you sleep on my baby, because the sign of this storm, is not, good. Get comfy." Knox mentioned when the whole team of nine entered the opening under the snowy slope hill, which was like an ant on the humongous mountain, the actual Mount Upaithric.

Caprice and Myra, who actually didn't like each other that much, shared a blanket that Knox handed out, because obviously there wasn't enough for everyone. Ruby and Gwyneth shared, Trent and Xavier shared, Ethan and Dylan shared, and Knox just slept in the corner of the little cave, by himself.

"This is weird," explained Ethan as he covered himself with the blanket, as Dylan did the same. "I always knew I was going to sleep with someone, but not with my best friend."

"You have no other choice, because I'm sure the girls don't want to get too cozy next to you guys, at this time." Knox laughed.

"True." the girls agreed.

Myra stared at the ceiling that was filled with hanging icicles, as she slept on the cold ground, sharing a blanket with her "frenemy". What if those sharp things fall on me in the middle of the night? Thought Myra.

Chapter 10

WAITING FOR ICE

"Sir, I am sure that we will find her." insisted Ernest the giant, with his dark features and hairy body. He was the chauffeur of the Rolls Royce Phantom that appeared gray in the sunlight. Mayor Mercury was sitting in the back seat of the luxurious car, with wrinkles forming under his dark eyes. The mayor had never been so worried, he told Buttercup before that he would take her with him to find Myra, but he didn't think she would know anyways, and the mayor didn't want to risk losing the girl. As hostage, Buttercup was perfect, because she seemed to be the only one that shined and smiled, so hopefully for the mayor, someone from the team will beg for her.

"Oh shut it, I'm calling home," snapped the mayor, "yes, Annalisa? Put the girl on the phone... Hello... Listen, Buttercup... Do you have a boyfriend or partner on the team by any chance...? If you tell me, I will free you... Tell me... Fine... Give me Annalisa... Whip her... Now... Harder... I demand the answer... Don't stop till she answers... Spit it out Buttercup... THANK YOU... Annalisa, stop whipping... No, keep her in there... Take care."

"So? Anything new? Boss?" asked Ernest.

"His name is... Trent." smirked the mayor.

The storm was alive, by the time Myra's eyes flashed open. She was covered in a thick blanket, lying on the floor of the cave. All her team members were asleep, all over the place, literally.

"When is it going to end?" smiled Ethan, enjoying the little light that made the rough storm morning. Myra hesitated at the surprising fright.

"I thought you were asleep," Myra said with a yawn, "don't know, it looks like it's gonna be a while."

"I woke up a couple of minutes ago, disappointed. But when I saw your pretty eyes open, I smiled." grinned Ethan, brushing his messy blond hair with his hands.

Myra giggled, and then got up, and walked to the opening of the cave. Heavy winds blew her strawberry blonde hair back. Large flakes of snow dropped to the white ground, as Ethan stood next to shivery Myra.

"I know this is a cliché, but, do you want my jacket?" Ethan laughed.

"Déjà vu. Sure," Myra enjoyed the feeling of Ethan's jacket covering her shaky shoulders, "awkward, hehe."

"Déjà vu, tell me about it," Trent mentioned from behind, "you could have just asked for mine."

"I think she prefers my, jacket." muttered Ethan turning to his teammate.

✳✳✳✳

"Found his number?!" asked the mayor, as he popped a stink bomb into a knocked out guard's open mouth. Mayor Mercury and Ernest were at the ProDyno headquarters, a cramped room at the top of a skyscraper, in Skullcrowth. Even though the mayor organized the team, he didn't want to cause any attention, so he took out the guards of the headquarter.

"Bliss. Dr. Jon Bliss. Where's your phone?" Mayor Mercury demanded, from the gray haired computer freak, which sat on a wooden chair, with a bright laptop on his lap.

"Mayor Mercury." the computer freak stood up to greet the mayor.

"Where is your phone?!"

"Here," Dr. Bliss handed his hundred year old flip phone, to Mayor Mercury. The mayor flipped it open, clicked a few buttons and then placed the phone on his ear.

"Trent? Is it... Hello... Answer... No need to know... I have your girlfriend... No, I want... You have to do me a favor..." said the mayor to the shaky voice, on the other side of the line. Dr. Bliss watched his boss, confused, then was even more confused when the giant that came with the mayor, dragged him out of the stink bomb-filled-room.

"You are very lucky, Jon." Sterling Gee Mercury mentioned to the computer freak, which made himself comfortable, in the backseat of the Rolls Royce Phantom, while Ernest drove the car. "You know why? Because I needed Trent's number, if you didn't give it to me, you could've died from the disgusting smell that was in that bomb. Thank me, Jon, thank me!"

"Thank you, Mr. Mercury, thank you."

"I thought so. Talk to your family, you'll be away with me for quite a long time. Ernest, call Harvey, we need him." barked Mayor Mercury.

Chapter 11

FROSTBITE

"EEEEWL!" yelled Gwyneth, staring at her frozen toes. "FROSTBITE?"

"I think so, they're hideous!" laughed Caprice Carter. They were still in the cave, and the snow storm was still alive. Knox Hartley stared with disgust at Gwyneth's disgusting toes, and then pulled out a medicine bottle from his bag. "Shut it, I'm sure behind those ugly boots, there are nasty feet that stink to death!" meowed Gwyneth.

"Grow up, Gertrude!" Caprice snatched the medicine bottle from the wise leader, yanked the lid off, and splashed it over Gwyneth's head. Gwyneth's mouth opened, as her auburn hair turned a nasty dark green color, and started shedding off her oval shaped head.

"You a** wipe!" purred Gwyneth, as she scratched Caprice's cheeks with her sharp blade-like nails. "Gertrude's my dead mother's name."

Caprice backfired a scratch back, before her team members pulled her away from the going-bald-Gwyneth that looked like a depressed mermaid with frozen toes.

Myra laughed at the entertainment, while Ruby helped calm down Gwyneth.

"It's gone, all gone!" Gwyneth scowled at the feeling of her bald head. "Thanks a lot Blondie."

"HAHAHAHAHAHAHAHAHAHAH," Myra giggled while covering her mouth, "sorry, Gwen."

"AAAAAAAA, give me a towel, or scarf." Gwyneth roared. Once her hair was covered, she sat in the corner alone, trying to hide her face.

"Wow, girls do really look bad when they're bald," said Ethan blankly.

"Shut up." Ruby gave Ethan a punch on the shoulder.

By the next day, the ice that covered Gwyneth's toes vanished, due to Gwyneth actually trying the left over medicine, warming her toes, a lot, and taking a few pills. But, instead, Ruby was found with severe frostbite, the next morning.

"I... I... I... ummm..." Knox shivered when Ruby asked if he had any frostbite treatment left. "I am so sorry... I... No more, there is no more. Listen, put on some mittens, and warm them."

Ruby tried warming herself, but with the storm that didn't end yet, it was a challenge. Even with all the blankets around her, she was still freezing.

"Everyone! Get up!" Knox Hartley made his team wake up from their sleep; it was five days after Ruby got the severe frostbite. "Get out of here! Now!"

Myra and all her teammates, except Ruby, and Knox, rushed outside the cave and into the storm. In ten minutes, Knox showed up alone.

"Where's Ruby?"

"She's... ummm... ummm... she is gone. The frostbite was too severe, she is gone." Knox shed a guilty tear. "If only I fetched more treatment, and kept her warmer."

"You're just going to leave her here?! How?! What is wrong with you?!" bald Gwyneth demanded, as she ran back towards the cave. But, Knox blocked her way, and told her it was their only choice.

"What, if, what if she's still alive?" Gwyneth gulped. She pushed the team leader out of her way and rushed into the cave. In the corner of the icicle filled cave, lied Ruby with three blankets wrapped around her. When Gwyneth got closer to her best friend, she pulled out the blankets and, planted on the middle of Ruby's chest, was an icicle.

"You... KILLED HER!" Gwyneth pulled out her katar dagger, and started swinging it at Knox. But Knox blocked the swings, and took the katar dagger from her hand.

"I would never do such a thing! I found her like this when I woke up, and if I told you guys you would possibly think it was me. Plus, the severe frostbite didn't help her survive, trust me," mentioned Knox Hartley, handing back the katar dagger to the scared Gwyneth. Gwyneth rolled her eyes, and then placed her ear on Ruby's heart, checking if she was still alive.

The storm was ending, but it was still tough for the ProDyno team to get up Mount Upaithric, which felt even higher than Mount Everest, in their point of view.

"This is too much pressure," Knox said with stress, as he jumped over hard stones that were stuck to the mountain floor and sides, "we didn't reach the tower yet, and we already lost three members!"

"Well, I'm not surprised. Things can get tough here." mentioned Dylan with his posh accent.

Chapter 12

THE CIGARETTE CLUB

Mayor Mercury, Ernest, and Dr. Jon Bliss entered the repulsive building with pockets full of pistols. It was a famous nightclub that was always packed with all sorts of mischief people.

"Is Harvey, here?" Mayor Mercury asked the buff bodyguard that blocked the room's door. The room wasn't any room. It was where Harvey did all his business. He was owner of the nightclub, The Cigarette Nightclub, but only because his brother Sterling, bought it for him.

"Sir," the bodyguard flinched from his position in front of the door, and made way for the mayor and his help. Although the nightclub was ear-ripping from noise, Harvey's room, or "office", as he called it, was very, very quiet. Until the mayor and his help, came in.

"Harvey." said Mayor Mercury as he barged into the cramped room. It was a tiny room with little windows, a desk, a massage chair, an expensive rug, and a mini fridge. Harvey Mercury was relaxing on his massage chair, with a stripper on his lap. They were smooching, and it didn't look appropriate because the stripper was mostly nude, unlike Harvey who was in a tuxedo. "What are you doing?!"

"Sapphire, get off me!" said Harvey pushing the bleach haired stripper, off his lap. "Hello, brother."

"Harvey, get ready, we're going to find Myra. She is missing," demanded the mayor to his younger brother.

"I can't, I'm too in love to go anywhere, wait... what? Myra's gone?" grinned Harvey Mercury. Harvey had similar features to his brother; salt and pepper hair, dark eyes, and bushy eyebrows.

"I won't bother to tell the cops, until I'm desperate. But I am not worried, since I have Bliss and Ernest." the mayor introduced his bodyguard, and the computer freak to his drunk brother.

"Babe, don't go anywhere, I'll miss you." mentioned Sapphire while giving her boss a smooch.

"Get changed, you're coming with me, and so is Heather." replied Harvey as he got out of his chair and started getting ready to leave. Sapphire on the other hand left the room, apparently to get "Heather" and a coat.

Heather was a stripper too. Unsurprisingly Harvey had two girlfriends because of his big pocket of donated money, and important position in town, as "the mayor's brother". But what was unusual was that Heather, Ernest, Dr. Bliss, and the mayor were the only ones that actually left the night club. Harvey said he had "business" with Sapphire, and would catch up later.

"Stop staring at me, you desperate freak," scowled Heather at Dr. Bliss, who kept looking at Heather's chest. Heather's hair was black with red tints, and her eyes were sparkly and matched her half nude outfit.

"What a bastard, he sent me you instead of bothering to come himself," cursed Mayor Mercury, directly talking to Heather, who sat next to him with Dr. Bliss, in the back seat of the Rolls Royce Phantom, "do you want a knife, or pistol?"

"Both. Anything can come in handy," Heather answered after the mayor explained his daughter's story, "so, we're going to look for her, but we're still waiting for info from this guy, who apparently you have his girlfriend as hostage?"

"Pretty much. The weapons will only come in handy, if... OH SHIT! Why the f*** didn't Knox send her back, till now? He works for me, I don't work for him! What guts he has to keep her," fumed the mayor. "Heather, you and Bliss have a suite waiting for you at the top of Mount Upaithric Hotel. Ernest and I will see you in the morning."

Sapphire Wesley stepped on to the stage. She was ready for some pole dancing, private pole dancing, only for Harvey Mercury, who apparently was enjoying himself. Suddenly, Harvey's phone rang, and Sapphire watched as he left the huge nightclub area of the crappy building.

"Hey, listen, ask her for more bucks, before it's too late and her father shows up," barked Harvey into his phone, when he shut the door to his room/office. Sapphire came right behind him, although it was midnight, the couple enjoyed each other's company.

"Who was that? Baby?" asked Sapphire curiously, to Harvey, when he finished his phone call.

"Not important, I have no time for questions, let's go home."

"Heather, Heather, Heather. You will never ever work for my foolish brother until I die!" shouted Harvey Mercury into his phone. Heather had told him Mayor Mercury had offered her a lot of money to help him get his daughter. "Very well, Heather Aqua-Evans, you'll see."

It was 10:00 AM in Mount Upaithric, where Heather woke up with bright eyes. And, Dr. Jon Bliss wasn't there to protect her when the mob of Harvey and Sapphire barged into the hotel suite.

Chapter 13

BAD BUCKS

Myra Mercury was confused when the team leader headed to her with a grin. The ProDyno team was sitting in a failure of an igloo, close to the top of Mount Upaithric, where apparently the "last wizard in the world", lived. Myra was outside in the light snow storm that was about to die, and so was Knox Hartley.

"So, Myra, how are your thoughts on this quest, with the ProDyno team?" questioned Knox with his ear to ear grin.

"Ok, I guess," Myra rubbed her hands together for warmth. "What are you doing?"

Knox walked closer to the shivering mayor's daughter. "Remember, Myra? All those dollars that you gave me? Well, you better give me some more, or I'm taking you back."

Myra's face was blank, but when Trent jumped out of the igloo, and charged at the wrinkled full-of-experience Knox. Trent wrapped his arm around Knox's neck and tightened his grip, like he was trying to take all the breath out of the middle aged man, and said; "The only place Myra is going, is with me. I'm not letting Buttercup suffer more as a hostage."

Knox pushed Trent away and pulled out his shotgun, aiming at Trent's head. Trent didn't notice it coming, but didn't notice Ethan go behind Knox and whack him out with his war-hammer, either.

"That was close, he was like, gonna kill you... why?" Ethan emitted.

"None of your business," said Trent with relief. "Now leave, I want to talk to Myra."

Myra nodded, so Ethan walked into the igloo. Trent marched to Myra, "I beg you, please just come with me. I just can't live without Buttercup."

"Let me guess, my dad got your number and called you, didn't he?"

"Yup, so please..."

"Fine, but tomorrow morning,"

"Help me take this old man," Myra helped Trent drag knocked-out-Knox away from the igloo, "he'll bleed to death, and you shouldn't feel sorry because he was going to rob you."

"But we can't just leave him there, I... ummm," Myra said with guilt. "I..."

"Just come on, it's better for both of us."

Chapter 14

LIPSTICK STAINS

"Heather Aqua-Evans," grinned Harvey Mercury as he and Sapphire walked into the large suite. They told the front desk they were visiting Heather, so Harvey and Sapphire easily got upstairs, to the top floor of the Mount Upaithric Hotel, and easily barged in the suite. "Remember, a year ago, when you begged me for a job?"

Heather was sitting on a comfy couch in the suite's sitting room, and she was kind of nervous, when she saw her ex-boss march in. Heather's mouth was stuffed with a brown cigar, and she was still in her night gown.

"You loved me so much, but then betrayed me for some mayor dimwit, who had some extra bucks in him," scowled Harvey as he snatched the cigar from Heather's mouth, and stuffed it in his.

Sapphire pulled out lipstick and painted Heather's face with it. Heather pummeled a slap, but Sapphire grabbed Heather's arm, and twisted it till she heard it crack. Then, Heather pulled on Sapphire's bleach hair, till a lock of hair ripped out of her head.

"Ukhh," Sapphire yelped in pain. Harvey planted the cigar into Heather's nose, which caused an instant reaction and scream from scared Heather.

"So, do you change your mind?" Sapphire's elbow met Heather's nose.

"Over my dead body!" Heather kicked Sapphire on her private part, and then aimed her pistol at the couple. "Get out, or else..."

Harvey and Sapphire rushed out the suite, only to find Dr. Jon Bliss in front of them.

"How are you doing Mr. Mercury?"

"Get out of my way, you nerd," Harvey rolled his eyes and zoomed past the confused computer freak, with Sapphire on his tail.

Dr. Bliss had asked Heather what had happened between her and the couple, but Heather just shook her head and said they were thugs.

At 2:00 PM, Heather and Dr. Jon Bliss entered a Rolls Royce Phantom that was waiting for them in the hotel's driveway. Inside the spacious car was Ernest in the driver's seat, and Mayor Mercury in the back, wearing an expensive and elegant suit.

"We are going to meet my maid, Annalisa, at the Ice Plaza Winter Festival, for lunch; there is business to talk about."

There was no one, nothing, not even a tiny little mouse to keep Buttercup Archerson, company. She was still locked up in the basement bedroom, in the Mercury Villa, back in Skullcrowth. She wished that Trent would show up one day and rescue her, but it never happened. Why did I agree to trade lives with that Myra girl? Thought Buttercup.

All Buttercup was doing was sobbing, and drinking juice boxes and canned food that Annalisa the maid had stored in the bedroom, before she left to Mount Upaithric.

Chapter 15

A Mistake

Morning had passed, with Trent getting all grumpy that Myra disagreed to go back to Skullcrowth.

"You said that you would go in the morning, and yet we are still here!" said grumpy Trent.

"We can't leave just yet, we have to be with Ethan when he says to the others that we killed Mr. Hartley," answered Myra, "he is dead, right?"

"When everyone was asleep, he was still unconscious, so I killed him with my falchion," Trent mentioned, "by the way, who cares about Ethan, we have to go, before it's too late and Buttercup gets killed by your father."

"You did what? Huh?" Xavier asked as he popped out of the igloo. Myra and Trent were talking in the same place they did the night before, where Knox Hartley was also killed.

"Were you eavesdropping?" Trent frowned. "After all I did for you, and helped when your leg was injured."

"I didn't mean t…"

"Save it, X. You found out, Mr. Hartley is dead,"

"Why the f****** hell did you kill him?"

"That isn't important; now, go tell the others, Myra and I are leaving,"

At the same moment, Ethan and Gwyneth had come out from the igloo. Ethan was shocked and then questioned Myra why she was leaving with Trent.

"My father..."

"Shhh, you don't have to explain anything, Myra, let us go!" Trent grabbed Myra's arm and started dragging her away from the igloo.

"She doesn't want to go!" Ethan grabbed Myra's other arm to the igloo. "Let go!"

Myra looked to one side, at Trent's blue eyes, and then looked to the other side, at Ethan's dark eyes.

"I don't want any of you!"

The two teens backed away from the furious Myra. "LEAVE ME."

Myra yanked out her bow & arrow, and then closed her eyes as she pointed it in the middle of the two guys. Suddenly, Myra pointed her weapon to the right, and, the arrow stroke into the air.

Chapter 16

THE WINTER FESTIVAL

Annalisa O'Orton wore a classy gown and diamond earrings to the Ice Plaza Winter Festival. Annalisa was a maid who worked for Mayor Mercury, and as a maid, Annalisa was making quite a lot of money.

Raindrops splashed onto Annalisa's black umbrella as she marched into the Ice Plaza, a wide glass mall that swarmed with the rich and famous.

"Good day, sir," Annalisa shook her boss's hand.

"Hello, Annalisa," Mayor Mercury replied. The mayor's arm wrapped around Heather's shoulders. "This is Heather; she is going to be helping us..."

"Nice to meet you, Lisa," giggled the drunken Heather. "Why are your eyes so close together? You look like a donkey."

Annalisa frowned, and stroke her thin brown hair, like she didn't care.

Once Dr. Jon Bliss and Ernest came with truckloads of caviar on 24 karat gold plates, the sophisticated group sat in the V.I.P section, on a round white coated table.

"Ok, so, Hartley's phone is closed, and there is no sign of Trent, who is the savage girl's boyfriend," mentioned Mayor Mercury.

"Yes, sir."

"I want you, Annalisa, to visit my brother, Harvey, and eliminate his girlfriend from his life. And then talk him into helping me find Myra." said Mayor Mercury.

"Me??? I... ummm... I can't... I can't... eliminate... ummm,"

"I'll do it!" laughed drunken Heather, taking another sip of whisky.

"You? It won't work, Heather, you have too much history with Harvey, and his girlfriend."

"Do I? Do I really?"

It wasn't a good thing, to lose a loved one, but Myra didn't know what got into her. Ethan had died in her arms, with the bloody arrow that she killed him with. The arrow had dived into his heart, and silenced him, and then, he died.

"Why didn't you kill me? WHY? WHY NOT ME?" asked the guilty Trent, when it happened. Myra just sobbed, and then realized that she killed Ethan purposely.

Chapter 17

MEOW AND WOOF

Heather walked behind the clueless Sapphire with five eyes. Sapphire Wesley had just finished a full-of-spirit speech about how successful the winter festival was, every year. Harvey Mercury was with her but then disappeared in the crowd.

Sapphire marched up a flight of stairs, then turned right, and headed to a little balcony. While Heather was close behind, making sure the bleach haired stripper didn't notice her. Eyes shining, Sapphire stopped once she stepped into the dark sky of the tiny balcony. A windy breeze blew back Sapphire's hair as she heard footsteps behind her.

"Hello," laughed Heather Aqua-Evans.

As soon as Sapphire turned to face the familiar voice, Heather rammed her off the balcony rail. Heather grinned at the sight of Sapphire sinking down into the Ice Plaza garden.

"Happy now? Ms. Heather?" woofed a squeaky voice behind the happy Heather.

It was Annalisa O'Orton, with her fingers coiled around a wooden bat. Heather bit her lower lip, and then put her hands on her wide hips.

"What do you want, Lisa? Is it?"

"Annalisa," corrected Annalisa. "If you didn't insist, I could've finished her off myself and got rewarded a few bucks."

"I didn't know you were such a peasant,"

"Bye bye, Ms. Heather, I hope I don't ruin the Botox on your face." meowed Annalisa.

"You wouldn't dare touch me, you don't have the guts!"

"You are mistaken, dear,"

"Oh really?"

"Yes, really!" Annalisa charged at Heather, and the wooden bat met Heather's head two times until she fell to the floor and got beaten up even more.

Chapter 18

Desperate Again

Buttercup Archerson's eyes opened, to a dark, new day, in Skullcrowth. The teenager got out of bed and started banging on the bedroom door, for the hundredth time, that week.

"HELP!!! HELP!!! GET ME OUT OF HERE!!! TRENT?! ARE YOU THERE?! HELLO?!" yelled Buttercup with tears. But no one answered, and nothing moved. Buttercup just sat on the edge of the bed, and stayed there like a statue.

After a while, Buttercup got out of place, and for the first time realized that she never checked the cabinet drawers. In the top drawer, that Buttercup yanked open was: nothing. While the second drawer was filled with: action figures, a file of lined paper, comic books, and a stack of CDs. Otherwise the last drawer had piles of pens and pencils.

"B**** used to draw," whispered Buttercup with a giggle. Then, the dyed black haired teenager ripped out a piece of paper, from the notebook, and grabbed a pencil. After that, she spilled out all the words in her mind, onto one of the blank pages, of the scribbled notebook.

Buttercup wrote:

I'm sorry baby, forgive me. I have no other choice, but you should be happy for me, it isn't like I was that happy, anyways. If you find this, keep it as a memory, not as a treasure. Love you.

Xoxoxoxo,

Buttercup Archerson.

Chapter 19

WHY?

"His death killed me, but your urge to save Buttercup, brought me back to life," Myra Mercury flipped back her strawberry blonde hair, that made a huge contrast with her hair's dark roots.

"So... you killed him on purpose? Instead of me?" asked Trent.

"No s***, f***tard," snapped Gwyneth, trying to comfort Myra with her words of wisdom, "can't you tell?"

Most of the ProDyno group was outside of the igloo, where Knox Hartley had got killed, and the snow storm had stopped. Xavier and Trent stood there, watching Gwyneth, Myra, and dead Ethan, who were on the cold ground. Ethan's body stretched out disgustingly with blood floods everywhere. While Myra and Gwyneth were on their knees, right next to him.

"Harsh, huh? Ethan was really cool. Did you really have to kill him?" uttered Xavier. "I mean he doesn't have a family, so..."

"SHARRAP!" interrupted Gwyneth.

"What?! No, family? Ethan's an orphan?!" Myra yelled.

"No...Ummm.... yes, all of us, in fact... most of us... are orphans," Trent blurted out. "Okay! You think that we have loser families that don't care if we die or not? Well, you're wrong because we... had, loving families."

"I... had... a... twin." said Gwyneth, remembering memories. "But..."

"I, never... knew..." Myra sobbed more. "What happened?"

"All of us have a story." gasped Xavier.

Gwyneth started crying too, and then Myra exploded. Xavier popped back into the dark igloo, and Trent followed.

"What the... hell." questioned Xavier and Trent as they saw the most random thing. In front of them, was Caprice and Dylan, smooching intensely.

As soon as the two guys freaked out, the unknown couple let go of each other, then, smiled.

"What? You never seen people kiss?" laughed Caprice Carter.

"Awkward, I know. I thought Capri wasn't my cup of tea, either, but I was mistaken," Dylan smirked.

"Cup of tea? Ethan just got killed, and you guys are kissing all over the place?"

"Life goes on; you think I still miss those retards, Prissy and Alexia? Hahaha!"

"Wow, as cold blooded as you are, I still love you to crumpets!" said Dylan, ignoring the fact that his best friend just got killed.

"You know that English stereo type, with crumpets and tea? Well, you aren't helping, dude." answered Xavier.

Trent rolled his blue eyes, and then left the icy igloo.

Chapter 20

BRUISES AND BASTARDS

Heather was in bed, just lying there, wanting to go out and breathe some fresh air.

"I gotcha some hot chocolate," Dr. Jon Bliss handed a mug of flaming hot chocolate, to the bored Heather. Dr. Bliss was in his casual nerdy clothes and glasses, as he sat on the edge of Heather's bed, expecting a kiss or thank you.

"Eewl! Chocolate? Seriously? I'm not a big fan of fat, and especially, hot chocolate." roared the grumpy Heather, as she pushed the mug away, making it spill onto Dr. Bliss's clothes.

"HOT!!!" the computer freak threw his mug backwards, making it crash to the hotel suite floor, and grabbed Heather by her tank top collar. "What does it take to impress you?!"

"Sick packs, money, and cars!" Heather high fived Dr. Bliss's face, and then took her coat and left the suite.

The computer freak followed her to the front driveway of the hotel, and jumped into the Rolls Royce Phantom (that the mayor used 24/7), after her.

"IS SHE GONE? Sapphire Wesley? IS SHE DEAD?" demanded Mayor Mercury, staring disgustingly at Heather, and the bruises all over her body.

"I think?"

"You think?"

"See, Mayor Mercury, if you assigned me the job in the first place, Sapphire would've gone for sure," Annalisa pointed out.

"Ernest! Get a move on, you nosey brat," the mayor rolled his eyes. The Rolls Royce Phantom sped away triumphantly, from the other cheaper cars that sat on the driveway, waiting for passengers.

"Hello brother!!!" Harvey Mercury shouted at the phone. He was at the Mount Upaithric Motel, simply just because it was cheaper than the Mount Upaithric Hotel, and not too close to his brother, Sterling.

"Yes, Harvey, which room are you in?" Mayor Mercury questioned. The mayor and Heather were visiting Harvey and Sapphire, who was apparently still alive.

The room that the couple was in was crap. It had old furniture, hairy bathrooms, tiny windows, but, it surprisingly had more than three rooms. While Harvey was in the old 70's styled kitchen, preparing glasses of lemonade, Mayor Mercury and Heather sat quietly on the chipped off green couch.

"Are you guys comfortable?" asked Harvey from the kitchen.

"Yeah, I'm just going to use the bathroom," Heather got up, and vanished at the turn, that led to the bedroom hallway. There were two doors on the left, and one straight ahead. But before Heather could try a knob, someone's hand covered her move with force, from the back. She tried to scream, but nothing came out, so she finally couldn't fetch any more oxygen, and fainted.

Harvey Mercury finally marched to the little sitting room, and placed a glass of pee-like lemonade, on the coffee table.

"Please try it, dear brother," grinned Harvey Mercury. "I made this with happiness."

The mayor reached for the glass, grasped it tightly in his hand, and gulped down a few mouthfuls of the bitter liquid. "This is very light, I must say. What is in it?"

"Lemons, sugar, and some, sleeping pills," Harvey said smartly.

"Sleeping pills? What the f*** is wrong with you? Why?!" demanded Sterling Mercury.

"Wait for it…" A glass vase crashed to the back of Mayor Mercury's head, sending him down to the ground, with a thump.

Chapter 21

CLUELESS

Ultranne McUltra, Myra's best and richest friend, with her ear length pink hair, was at Buttercup's farmhouse. It was on sale, since Buttercup's only relative on the planet, her brother, Trevor, decided that since Buttercup had disappeared, there was no need to keep the farmhouse.

"LOL. This is so cheap, I probably need even more closet space, but this is good enough," smirked Ultranne from her fancy Mercedes Benz sports car, as she stared at the small farmhouse. There was a wooden sign planted into the ground, next to the farmhouse's front door, that said: *On sale for $250,000. Furniture included.*

When the elegant car finally sped away, it didn't stop until it landed in the Mercury Villa's circular driveway. Ultranne's huge disco heels clacked on the rough ground, as she exited her sports car, and headed to the red roofed villa. Sparkly and pink, Ultranne's nails knocked on the neat front door.

"Excuse me, ma'am, I have the keys, but I'm afraid you can't go in. No one's allowed until the boss returns," said a bald guard who had glanced at Ultranne, uncomfortably.

"Is that saw so?" Ultranne hissed. She scratched his round face, and then twirled in the air, unleashing a high kick that knocked the guard, a few feet backwards. "Give me that, you unpleasant moron."

Ultranne McUltra snatched the keys from the guard's palm, and entered the villa with triumph.

The villa was in no shape, literally. It was pathetic to Ultranne, how poorly the living room looked. Dust filled the area, and antiques appeared more bland than usual. The young millionaire dashed around the villa, searching for any human being, to tell her what was going on.

Finally, Ultranne grabbed a glass vase, when she heard footsteps. A tall sneaky guard appeared from out of the blue with a pistol up his ass, literally.

"Not again," Ultranne sighed. "Don't get near me, freak."

The guard laughed, and then ducked at the vase throw that Ultranne thought was going to work.

"You are beautiful." The guard walked to the frightened Ultranne, and sexually harassed her.

Chapter 22

AWKWARD MOMENTS

Myra Mercury sat quietly in the shivering space, listening to Gwyneth, whose hair had grown a little, but dark colored instead of auburn.

"You're really ugly hair reminds me of my mother," mentioned Myra.

"What the hell? You call your mom, ugly?" said Gwyneth. "Oh, wait, where is your mom?"

"Dead. Gone. Ugly. Buried. From... CANCER!" sobbed Myra.

"I'm so..."

"Shut up, you aren't sorry. You think, or should I say thought, that my life was perfect, but you are wrong."

"Why do you call your mom ugly, Myra?"

"Because I hated when she was bald, or had short hair! Plus, she never wore her $80,000 ring, that my..."

"Give me a break, princess, that is why you hate your mom?"

"Yes, Gwyneth, because she left me!" Myra zoomed out of the igloo, bumping into Trent, who was going to enter the igloo.

Trent rubbed his frostbite face, and looked at Myra's lush-like features, which made the cold, burning hot. Myra pushed him out of her way, and started running uphill. Trent went after her, with worry.

The two teenagers hiked up Mount Upaithric, in silence, once Trent caught up to Myra.

"What happened, Butter-Myra?"

"You were goanna call me Buttercup?"

"I...miss her...but, I also like you, Myra Mercury." Trent stopped, and squished Myra's hand, with his own.

Chapter 23

BLEACH BITS

Tired and confused, Heather Aqua-Evans lay on a hideous bed, with pink and purple linens, and a roaring fireplace. But, Heather's head wasn't on the bed; it was on Sapphire's knee, where Heather's hair was being bleached.

"Get off me!" Heather blurted angrily.

"No, you get off me!" replied Sapphire Wesley, with her weak appearance. Sapphire had a creamy cast wrapped around her leg, staples on her head, and a runny nose.

Heather walked to the mirror, in front of the narrow bed, and stared at her bleach painted hair, with disgust. "Whatcha do to my hair, you retard?!"

Sapphire threw the brush clasped in her dry palm, backwards, and laughed. "Did you say goodbye to your old boyfriend? He's out, at the moment."

"Huh? Oh… WHERE IS MAYOR MERCURY?"

"Hehe. Asleep, locked in a bedroom, like you," giggled Sapphire. "You'll get out when the mayor and his crew are all dead."

"Really? I don't want to end up like the girl Sterling captured," Heather nudged the door knob, of the dim bedroom, but it didn't budge.

"You're gonna have to try harder than that,"

A bang BANGED at the wooden door, and it didn't sound like a sane person. "Heather? Are you there?"

"HEL…"

Ultranne was devastated, when she finally was done handling the guard that tried raping her. The tall guard's body sunk into the kitchen sink, when Ultranne slapped him across the room.

"Now, where was I?"

The young millionaire trotted downstairs, to an unorganized basement. The lounge, with its funky colors was dark and unseen. But, lights came from the bedrooms, which stood in a line, in front of Ultranne. Ultranne couldn't help but pound on the lighted bedrooms.

Chapter 24

The Remaining

The remaining of the ProDyno team hiked up the rough surface, with exhaustion. Xavier nagged with his one and a half leg, his arm around Dylan's shoulders, for support. Gwyneth's hair was coal colored, and her eyes glowed like pearls, as sunlight hit her eyes. While Caprice Carter, with her pale platinum blonde hair, was dreading the whole quest.

"I promise, I'll come with you, after we get that fat a** wizard," Myra told the athletic looking Trent, as they climbed over huge stones that blocked their way uphill. Unlike the tropical jungles, which were far south from Skullcrowth, Mount Upaithric was bland and super steep. So steep, that Caprice slipped more than once, thanks to the wooden heels she nailed to her leather and fur boots, a few days ago.

Further ahead, a pile of snowballs, **humongous** snowballs, lay there, silently. But in seconds, the sound of a shotgun blurted out of nowhere. And, the snowball pile tumbled down. Trent shoved Myra and Caprice out of the way, causing them to stumble down the mini hill. And, Gwyneth pressurized the handicap Xavier down the hill, too. While Dylan got squashed by the monstrous snowballs, all alone.

Chapter 25

YOURS TRULY

The weather splashed with colors, when the sun decided to set. A faint red sky was no match for Annalisa's full red lips.

Annalisa O'Orton slipped into an open window, of Harvey Mercury's motel room, with confidence. Her hair was combed back, her brows were marked with darkness, and her eyelashes were blackened.

"Who are you?! Get out! Immediately!" gasped Harvey Mercury at the look of the bold Annalisa. Whip in hand; Annalisa whacked Harvey with strength, sending his oval face to the side, and his nose drip with ketchup-like blood.

"Bye, bye, Mr. Harvey Mercury," grinned Annalisa. Who with no second thoughts destroyed Harvey's private part, with a hard kick.

Heather was standing at the bedroom door, when it whistled open, revealing an unrecognizable Annalisa.

"Get the mayor. I'll take care of that bimbo, Sapphire."

Sapphire Wesley's hair was sucked into the toilet, when Annalisa walked in. Annalisa pulled on Sapphire's head roughly, until the bleached hair cut off the hungry toilet, and Sapphire spun around with rage.

"That pathetic b**** pushed me, and then flushed my coiffured hair down the…"

"Put a fig in it, Sherlock," Annalisa pounded Sapphire's stomach with her fist, and then butt headed her, sending her down to the bathroom rug, where the back of her head hit the toilet seat.

Harvey Mercury was sitting on a torn couch, when Annalisa and confused Mayor Mercury, headed for the front door.

"I see Lisa really hurt you, brother," chanted the mayor, when he noticed his brother's hands were on his aching private part. Harvey wanted to stop them, but he was in too much pain.

"You wanted me asleep? Huh? You want my daughter? You want my money? Over my dead body!" the mayor took out one of his signature stink bombs, and made it fly into the air, hit the ceiling, and land like an acorn on Harvey's head.

"I just don't get it, why would he do this to me?" the mayor asked himself, when he, Heather, Ernest, Annalisa, and Dr. Jon Bliss were cramped in the Rolls Royce Phantom, that even shined in the transition of sunset to night.

"I never liked him, sir, he always talked bulls***." Mentioned Ernest from the driver's seat.

"Money is most people's best friend, Mayor Mercury. Isn't it? Heather?" questioned Annalisa with triumph.

Heather stared blankly at the happy Annalisa, who was sitting on the other side, in the back seat of the fancy car (the mayor in between).

"Yeah, she told me the other…" Dr. Jon Bliss started, from the passenger seat, but got hushed by exhausted Heather.

"Give me a break, Bliss, if someone offered you a million bucks to assassinate Harvey, wouldn't you do it?"

"I would do it if they didn't give me a million bucks, anyway,"

"How generous of you. Now, get ready, tomorrow we're all going to the actual Mount Upaithric, and no one's getting in our way." Mayor Mercury replied.

Chapter 26

ASIAN PRINCESS

Slanted dark eyes stared at the sleepy Harvey Mercury. The lady in front of him was Asian, her hair so black it looked purple, and her skin a mixture of yellow and white. She was simply beautiful. The lady's black hair was curled into pigtails, and she was wearing sparkly casual clothes.

"Are you okay, sir?" asked the Asian lady, with a perfect English accent. Harvey Mercury realized he was in his motel room, lying comfortably on the sitting room couch.

"Yes, fine, how... who..."

"I'm Kimmie Julie Woo, I work as the motel clerk, remember?"

"Then how did you get in? And why are you in your casual clothes?" Harvey sat straight, and then crossed his arms.

"It's my break. I just saw smoke, and came to check what happened. News flash, you have to leave the motel," said Kimmie Woo.

"Listen, Miss Kimmie. We need more time,"

"Then pay up,"

"First help me find my girlfriend," Harvey walked out of the sitting room, with Kimmie on his tail, searching the bedrooms and bathrooms.

Sapphire Wesley laid dead on the bathroom tiles, with blood running out of her bashed head.

"What happened here?" sighed Kimmie.

"They killed her!!! Those b******!!!"

"She might have just slipped and hurt her head," Kimmie pointed out. "Wait... whose 'they'."

Kimmie was happy when Harvey told her he was against his brother, the mayor, because quite frankly she never liked the mayor, either.

"Wait, since there was smoke, why didn't the dedicator..." Harvey got interrupted.

"It's been broken for years."

The two decided to take Sapphire's dead body to Bliquerdorf Sea, and throw her in, so no one would notice her death.

"Thanks for helping me, Miss Kimmie,"

"Kimmie*. No need for 'Miss'"

"Okay, Kimmie. Why did you help me? Huh?" Harvey said as he and Kimmie walked on the Bliquerdorf Sea shore, in the dark night, after demolishing Sapphire's body into the sea.

"Because, you're cute. And, I hate your brother, too. Lastly, the motel doesn't need any more bad news and problems."

"Would you like to go to dinner? Possibly at... Zoe's Zeafood?" blushed Harvey Mercury.

"Sure, why not?"

Chapter 27

SALT AND PEPPER

Platinum blonde haired Caprice Carter didn't give up. No matter how many times she slipped, she didn't give up, especially when she had to hike all over again after Trent rescued her and Myra from the storming snowballs.

Bruises and headaches filled Myra, when she had fallen. She was surprised that they were still alive, very surprised.

"We just fell like thirty feet, I'm sure we're in heaven," Gwyneth rubbed her forehead.

"Wait… where's Dylan?"

Dylan's back was partially broken when he landed roughly on the snowy ground, in the beginning of a little hill, in the Mount Upaithric actual mountain. More outrageous sized snowballs scrambled over Dylan, seconds after he fell.

"Is he still alive?!" screamed Caprice, running to her new boyfriend. Dylan's eyes were closed, but other than that the creamy snowballs didn't kill him, but the long fall might've. "Why does everyone I like always end up hurt or dead?"

"That isn't true," shivered Gwyneth.

"It is true! First Alex and Prissy, and now Dilly."

"Dilly? Seriously? Can't you give him a better nickname?" laughed Myra, while she helped Trent get Dylan off the ground. Dylan was still unconscious, so Gwyneth wasn't the only one helping a teammate up the hill, again.

When the team finally got up the hill again, with partially broken backs and headaches, they encountered a grotto.

"IS THIS REAL?! LIKE SERIOUS?! I'VE ALWAYS DREAMED OF THIS!! A PRIVATE SANCTUARY!!" Caprice chanted with delight. Caprice ripped off her leather armor and boots, revealing a bra and bikini, and then cannonballed into the circular pond, that fitted cozily in the beautiful grotto. Milliseconds, and Caprice floated back up the surface of the pond. Minutes, and the whole (remaining) ProDyno team relaxed in the bubbling pond, in their swimwear of course.

Myra's head rested on Trent's shoulder, Caprice's fingers had met with Dylan's, and Gwyneth's head was sunk into Xavier's chest. Other than the heavenly hot pond which was perfect for the freezing weather, the grotto was like a limestone cave that's ceiling were sprouted with stalactites that curled in its tips.

As Gwyneth attacked Xavier's neck with hickeys, Myra stared at the open grotto's rough walls and wondered what it felt like. So, she struggled out of the tight pond, into the cold air, and stroked the grotto wall. From the pond, Trent glanced at the attractive Myra that was wearing a glossy bikini and a strapless bra.

Caprice Carter was the only one outside the warm pond. This means she was the only one that scratched a long stalactite off the ceiling, with her tiny portable chainsaw to try to slay a polar bear, which appeared out of nowhere. Caprice tripped into the pond, on her way to the monstrous white bear, so the stalactite slipped into Myra's hands. Myra flipped her hair back, and walked confidently to the giant. The rest of the team crowded out the pond, letting

Xavier sneak a tube filled with lemonade green liquid, and spill it quickly into the bubbly pond.

The ProDyno team watched the pond turn a funky green, as Myra charged at the polar bear. She waved the stalactite into the bear's chest's direction, but the stalactite went through the bear's heart, without any harm. So, with one scratch from the bear's sharp nails, Myra's strapless bra got ripped from the middle, exposing her breast to the bear, and a ripped bra to the ground.

"HAHAHAHA!!!" Caprice exploded with laughter, causing Gwyneth to frown, and push her out of place. Caprice's head ended up right before the edge of the green pond, with the tips of her platinum blonde hair touching the pond, faintly.

Myra covered her breast embarrassed, and then started running away from the grotto, and most importantly away from the bear. Trent was the only other person there, capable of defeating the polar bear, because everyone else was slightly injured in a way. As muscular and strong Trent was, he was no match for the beastly polar bear, with bazookas as arms. And so, Trent flew into the air after one punch.

The polar bear marched closer to the grotto, where Caprice had gotten up, staring at the tips of her hair that was a lime green. She raged at the sight, and pulled out her mace. Caprice flew into the air, and swung the mace at the polar bear's head, sending him to the ground. The bear got up, again, but Gwyneth pulled out a perfume bottle and faced the animal. With three sprays, the grotto filled with an aroma, which made the polar bear dizzy. A poke from Dylan, and the polar bear fell backwards, into the steaming green pond.

"Thanks for the green dip dye," Caprice forced a smile at Gwyneth, after the polar bear had sunken down the green pond.

"Thanks for the bald head, and now this!" Gwyneth tugged on her short dark hair.

"I'm freezing," said Xavier as he hugged Gwyneth tightly. Dylan did the same to Caprice, and the team just stood there, in their swimwear, wondering where Trent and Myra were.

Chapter 28

PLANS

They made quite a couple, Dr. Bliss and Annalisa. He was smart looking, she was too. He wore glasses, she did too. He was crazy, she was crazy, too.

Annalisa had never driven a Rolls Royce before, but the mayor's Rolls Royce Phantom was quite fabulous. Plans were changed, and Dr. Bliss and Annalisa were asked to go back to Skullcrowth to check on Buttercup, plus if Myra had returned, or had **been** returned.

Heather, Ernest, and Mayor Sterling Gee Mercury had rented a yacht for their trip, in the Bliquerdorf Sea. They wanted to go find Myra, obviously, especially before Harvey tried to kidnap her for the money.

Chapter 29

ONLY CHILD

"It always sucked to be alone," said Myra Mercury. Myra and Trent had cuddled each other in the cold. And the worst part was they were both still in their swimwear, and **half** nude in Myra's case.

Trent was obviously shirtless but wore his knee-length swimming trunks, because that is what guys usually wear, when they go swimming. But, in Myra's case, she was only wearing her glossy bikini because the polar bear had ripped her strapless bra, and plus Myra had left her armor behind.

It was weird that Myra's breast was cramped into Trent, but, they were both cold and had no other choice.

"This is… awkward, but… it feels good," smiled Trent. After the polar bear had punched him, it literally made him fly.

"Yeah, it does," answered Myra with a cold giggle.

"So you don't know if you have siblings?" Myra questioned.

"No, but I remember that a long time ago, I used to… HUH! I think I do have…"

"Lucky. I was always alone,"

"Were you bullied?!" demanded the shocked Trent.

"No, most people liked me in school, and I had no real enemies, but…"

"But what?!"

"There was a dude… I dated him, and… when we broke up… he used to always p*** me off about how much fun it is to have siblings… and… you know!" stressed Myra, who got away from the confused but freezing Trent.

"Where are you going?! We were having a moment!!!" said Trent. But Myra had already walked away, topless again.

Chapter 30

FANGS

It was supposed to be a yoyo competition, but Ultranne McUltra and Chandler DeChan realized it wasn't, when they were the only people there, other than a mafia wearing tuxedos, in a huge center. The center was basically a center that people did parties in, but obviously the mafia didn't want to do a party.

Chandler DeChan was Myra's ex-boyfriend, who kept on blabbing about the **siblings'** thing, Myra was having problems with. Chandler was also a millionaire, by the way.

"Are you sure they're playing on us?!" whispered Chandler to Ultranne, before they were going to "yoyo battle" on stage.

"DUH! We're both rich, and we're the only people here that aren't wearing the same clothes!!!"

Right before the competition began; Chandler nodded his head at Ultranne's whisper, and then flashed his yoyo in the air. The cherry red yoyo circled and then rolled on the stage floor.

Ultranne swung her yoyo at a pale guy in a tuxedo, who looked like everyone else in the center, except Ultranne and Chandler. The vampires were attacking the young seventeen year old millionaires. How were they vampires? Well, the fangs of course.

The audience harassed too, but the millionaire's yoyo skills defeated at least half of them. A tall vampire crunched on Chandler's neck, but Ultranne's yoyo smacked him to his feet.

But, there was this one vampire that caught Ultranne's eyes.

Chapter 31

CRIES OF SADNESS

The ProDyno team was depressed. They were all in their leather armors again, but with solid frowns.

Caprice Carter was thinking about Preston, and how close they were, but then she remembered the shark gulp him down, so tears shed. Dylan was thinking about Ruby, and how much he liked her, until she got severe frostbite. Gwyneth was thinking about Alexia, and how much they hated each other, but she realized how much she missed her. While Myra was thinking about Ethan, who she fell in love with, he was like her dream boyfriend, except now that he was dead, she hugged herself tightly. Finally, Trent was feeling guilty how he killed the team leader, Knox Hartley, who he hoped was dead.

Otherwise, Xavier noticed how much his half leg had made him feel powerless, but with his teammates on his side, he didn't feel alone.

"I love you" was what the couples had told each other, before they started uphill again, hoping to finally reach the top, without another teammate dying.

Chapter 32

AGE GROUPS

Yves, Ultranne, and Chandler were in Ultranne's Mercedes Benz sports car, when a Rolls Royce Phantom crashed into the Mercedes's rear-end.

Yves Montgomery was one of the vampires that saved Ultranne from his vampire mafia mates. His hazel eyes matched his straight dark hair, and his pale white skin matched his clear white fangs. But his physical features wasn't only want Ultranne liked about him, it was also that he had saved her.

"I'm very sorry!" said Dr. Bliss, as he scrambled out of the scratched Rolls Royce Phantom. Yves got out of Ultranne's sports car like he was going to kill the man. And both Ultranne and Chandler had the same face, too. But Ultranne's frown turned into a smile, when she saw Annalisa get out of the Rolls Royce Phantom.

"LISA!!!" Ultranne ran into the maid's arms.

The middle aged maid giggled, and then started chatting with the seventeen year old millionaire. While Yves and Chandler faced the weak computer freak.

"What is wrong with you?! Grandpa?!" questioned the vampire.

"I apologize, son," said Dr. Bliss, in a small voice.

"We heard you the first time," Chandler gripped on Dr. Bliss's shirt collar, and then dug a fist into his stomach.

"NO!!! CHANDLER!!!" gasped Ultranne, pushing him away from the computer freak. Dr. Bliss got to his knees, but kept the pain inside him. Annalisa fumed, so she pinned Chandler to the ground, and started smacking him. Yves tried pulling her off him, but a huge wooden stick banged him, in the back of his head. The vampire struck to the ground, with Dr. Bliss with a wooden bat, behind him.

"Yves!" said Ultranne, as she kneeled down, to check if the three hundred year old teenage vampire was still alive.

By the time Yves woke up, and Annalisa stopped smacking Chandler, it was noon.

Annalisa and Ultranne sat in Zoe's Zeafood restaurant, in Skullcrowth, with three hurt men, by their side.

"Why didn't you tell me she was missing? I knew the Myra I went to the mall with seemed different." Ultranne mentioned, after Annalisa told her that Myra was missing.

"I miss... wait huh?" said the confused Chandler. "Is she missing, or did she run away?"

"Long story short, don't ever get near her again, boy, you broke her heart when you decided to break up with her!" Annalisa smacked the seventeen year old with triumph.

Chapter 33

BLACK DIAMONDS

The underground headquarters of the Black Diamond was dead silent when Ursula Van Duchess started her speech. She was the leader of the vampire mafia, the Black Diamond.

"My fellow vamps, I hope your hundred and thousand year old lives are fine, but we're here to talk about the millionaires and billionaires of Skullcrowth." Ursula uttered. Her white braids were coiled to the sides of her head, and her eyes were like pearls that shined 24/7. She was wearing a dark gown that flowed down the speech stand, she was standing on.

"Chandler DeChan and Ultranne McUltra hold 8.9 million dollars all together, which is quite a good amount for us to consume. And don't worry; we have someone already on their tail."

Chapter 34

Quartzite Plaza

The glass doors slid open for the three people to enter the spacious mall. With combed back hair and casual clothes, the teenage millionaire walked with his head held high. His friends were in their own world, staring at each other as they walked, realizing that they were meant to be together forever. It was Chandler DeChan, with Ultranne and Yves in their own world, of course.

The Quartzite Plaza mall was bubbly and bright, with narrow escalators that ascended to the mall's second floor. The two rich teenagers, with a vampire on their side who only **looked** teenage, climbed up the escalator to go to the food court.

"Chan, we're going to get some frozen yoghurt, go find us a spot," mentioned Ultranne to Chandler, when they reached the center of the food court. Chandler nodded and then began empty table searching.

Finally, he found a spot. It had metal chairs surrounding it, which were neatly tucked slightly under the table, but light, that was lighter than the mall's skylights, was becoming brighter.

Two what-looked-like teenage girls filled the area with a flowery aroma. They banged there $900 handbags on the circular glass table, and then gave a grin to Chandler. One girl had wavy hair that shined from the roots to the tips. The other had frizzy hair and long black eyelashes.

"Thank you," smirked the wavy haired girl as she took a seat, and was copied by her friend.

Chandler just stood there, yes, they were gorgeous, but Chandler wasn't going to let his friends down. "S…"

Chandler's mouth stopped talking when he saw something. The girl with the long eyelashes revealed her teeth, well, what mostly appeared was her plain white fangs. It came along with a hissing sound. Chandler turned, and wanted to leave but sharp nails dug into his arm.

"Where are you going, honey?"

"I…"

"SIT!" barked the frizzy haired girl, who appeared to have the claws.

Chapter 35

INDIGO

Silk outfits were quite unusual to wear to Mount Upaithric, right? I'm afraid Heather Aqua-Evans completely disagrees. She wore a silk dress, which was a dark indigo that matched her nails, and silk indigo boots.

All Mayor Mercury could see was indigo. Heather was the flower to his garden, the earth to his universe. And she looked damn impressive to him.

"Are you sure you'll make it uphill, without any trouble?" Ernest the giant asked the indigo covered woman.

"You fool, we're not hiking, we have these," Mayor Mercury yanked three elegant looking pens out his pocket. Unlike Heather who wore unsuitable silk, the two men were wearing climate friendly outfits.

After each of the three adults held a pen in their hand, Mayor Mercury pressed the top of his. His black and white pen expanded by height, and then by width, turning into a big square. The middle of the top of the big square lifted, revealing helicopter rotor blades. Mayor Mercury put the device above his head.

The blades started spinning, lifting the mayor off the ground and into the air.

The strawberry blonde dye was starting to fade on the top part of Myra's head, next to the roots. She sighed; with every step she took, wishing she was somewhere else. Her mother was the only person she was living for, but, not until the big divorce.

Sterling Gee Mercury wasn't always very open-minded and straight forward, but his wife, was. It wasn't exactly love at first sight, either. It was more like an arranged marriage. As beautiful as Myra's mother was, she wasn't what the mayor wanted in a women. He liked the types with the oversized breast, a big butt, and skin loads of Botox.

The mayor used to whack her with his whip, every time she annoyed him or complained about something. Yes, the whip that they used on Buttercup was the same the mayor used on his wife, who ran away after she gave birth to Myra.

"Babe, what's that indigo figure over there?" Myra asked Trent, when she looked back from her steep hike. Trent turned, with his messy hair that stunk and was way dirtier than it was, when Myra first saw him.

"Probably a bi…"

"DO YOU THINK IT'S THE WIZARD?!" pleaded Caprice Carter with excitement and relief. Caprice was going to run back downhill, but Dylan pulled her back upwards.

"I think it might be, but what do you think he would be doing all the way down there, if he lived all the way up there?" replied the exhausted Myra.

Chapter 36

HOME SWEET HOME

The Rolls Royce Phantom halted to a stop, once it reached the Mercury Villa's circular driveway.

Annalisa O'Orton and Dr. Jon Bliss exited the car, and stared at the beautiful home. Well, Annalisa did, while Dr. Bliss on the other hand glanced admirably at Myra's roofless Jaguar xk120, which was parked innocently at the side.

"WOW. This is like… A CLASSIC… FOR LIKE A TRILLION BUCKS!!!" yelled Dr. Bliss at the top of his lungs. "Can we drive it?! PLEASE!"

Annalisa dug her face into her palms, and took a deep breath. "We're here to check if Myra's returned, and check on how that peasant girl is doing. Not to ride…"

"Excuse me, Ms. O'Orton, but how did you get here? Where were you?" said a familiar voice. It was one of the guards.

The maid, who was also considered a house keeper, rolled her brown eyes and walked to the villa, to unlock the front door. Because of no result from Annalisa, the guard turned to Dr. Bliss, who was still admiring the roofless Jaguar classic. "And who are you? Are..."

The voice trailed off, as Annalisa left the front door ajar, and examined the first floor of the house, suspiciously. A few antiques were in pieces, but there was no Myra in sight, or even in sound. Plus although they left the poor Buttercup alone, with canned food and water, there was no voice of desperateness or begging.

In the kitchen, well, in the kitchen sink was supposedly some blood but...

Chapter 37

OCTOPUS AND KETCHUP! AGAIN

Harvey Mercury cherished memories of when he and his brother's family of three used to come eat at Zoe's Zeafood every week. But when he sat at the booth, alone, waiting for his new girlfriend who was supposedly in the restroom, he thought about Sapphire. Sapphire, with her bleached hair, and fake body parts, was still in his heart. He remembered when he dropped Sapphire into the beach, to sink down forever, with guilt.

But, now, at least he had Kimmie... Kimmie, who had reminded him of... his brother's wife. Yes, Myra's mother was from Asian origins but she was, like... a diamond, a Black Diamond.

Kimmie Julie Woo was in fact related, to Myra's mother, but quite faintly. Not because she was Asian too, but because Willamette Mercury's maiden name was Woo, too. Willamette, yes, was her name. The name of a mother, the name of a daughter, the name of a cousin, the name of a Black Diamond.

"Hello," smirked Kimmie as she marched back to the booth, and sat down, closely to Harvey, "so, what are you goanna order?"

"I already did," a waitress placed a plate of fresh octopus on the table, "May I have some ketchup, please?"

Chapter 38

ULTRANNE'S BASEMENT

Footsteps. Footsteps. Footsteps.

Chandler DeChan walked silently, on the tiled floor of the Quartzite Plaza's second floor. The second floor of the eerie mall consisted of a few shops, plus the food court. But compared to the food court, the other shops part was deserted.

A few feet behind walked two sneaky girls. Two very sneaky girls. In fact, vampires. The same girls that took Chandler's spot in the food court, and plus revealed their fangs.

Chandler could feel it. He could hear it. The irritating sound of high heels, very high heels. And then there was, the flowery aroma. So, the very smart Chandler got out a tiny gun, a very tiny gun. Well, not very tiny. He had found it back in Ultranne's basement. Her new "closet's" basement was stacked with all sorts of unusual weapons, which came "with" the place.

The gun was black, just black, and had... pretty much no bullets, but a hook, attached to a thick rope. Once you pulled the trigger, the hook would strike.

The two girls glanced at each other from minute to minute, waiting for the right time.

But, Chandler kept on fast walking, secretly. With the gun still in his hand. When Chandler finally came under an enormous skylight, he pulled the trigger.

Chapter 39

ICY ADVENTURES

Knox Hartley, yes, Knox Hartley, sat silently, with only ice. He was at the same cave the ProDyno team had used for shelter during the storm. Ruby's dead body was still there, under the blankets, probably decaying.

Knox had never felt so betrayed and broken. Well, he had the same feeling once, in middle school, when his crush told his enemy that she loved him. He was devastated, shocked. But after that, he just wanted revenge. Not from the guy, who was desperately in love with Knox's crush, too, but from the girl herself, Heather Aqua-Evans.

Knox remembered Heather, he had thought he almost saw her, flying with helicopter rotor blades, wearing indigo, outside. But obviously he was just, dreaming.

Rotor blades spun intensely as Heather flew higher into the sky. Her red tinted black hair was flying higher than her as she descended back to the bottom of the mountain, after the rotor blades had got chopped off from a crash.

Heather fell. She fell unconfidently, and scared. Something she never felt before. Maybe death. But no, it was too early, she was too young. Well, babe, this is life. When she hit hard on the bottom of the mountain, Ernest descended back down to the ground to help, but Mayor Mercury kept flying higher and higher.

Chapter 40

MORE RAILINGS

Chandler DeChan had gotten away before the two female vampires even thought about where he would've went. The one with frizzy hair got really mad that she almost pounded on a shop's glass, because of not finding Chandler, but instead she pounded her friend with her fist.

The wavy haired vampire friend covered her face with her long bony hand that was hiding under her sleeve. And with no second thought said, "How dare you hit me! It's not my fault the boy disappeared."

The frizzy haired vampire rolled her eyes, and whacked her friend again, but this time no second was spared for the wavy haired vampire to suck into her friend's neck with her fangs, and push her towards the second floor railing, that had a view of the first floor. Frizzy Hair tumbled backwards, and slipped over the railing.

Wavy Hair glanced at her new view, her old BFF lying on the first floor ground, with blood dripping from all sorts of places. Before anyone noticed the fallen vampire, wavy haired vamp dashed out of sight.

Chapter 41

DISTRACTED

A disturbing sound echoed into the modern kitchen of the Mercury Villa. Annalisa O'Orton was supposed to go downstairs to check on Buttercup, but she knew what was happening.

The tall slender guard was throwing punches at the newly bruised Dr. Bliss. Jon Bliss had accidently gotten into Myra's Jaguar xk120 for trial, so the guard dragged him out of the driver's seat and started teaching him a lesson.

Annalisa ran to the wrestling match, and hauled the guard off of the computer freak, with a frown.

"You kids are really f****** annoying!!!" Annalisa scowled, dragging Dr. Bliss across the concrete and to the Rolls Royce Phantom. The Rolls Royce Phantom powered out of the circular driveway with a bruised Dr. Bliss in the passenger seat, and an annoyed Annalisa driving.

Chapter 42

END OF EVERYTHING???

The ProDyno team finally marched onto a flat surface, at the top of Mount Upaithric. The mountain was so high, that clouds were quite closer than ever. View wise, the team could only see an ice covered Bliquerdorf Sea, but... there was a tall obsidian tower in front of them.

"This is it guys, the moment of truth!" Xavier chuckled as he leaned on the exhausted Gwyneth with one and a half legs.

"I have a good feeling that the wizard is going to be there. I'm 100% sure that he's here, I can feel It." smirked Myra with hope.

"Let's check." The ProDyno team trotted along a moss stone path to a 30 foot tall obsidian tower that belonged to apparently... The Last Wizard.

The front door of the tower was a cool birch wood that looked very heavy and sturdy. But that didn't stop them. Trent took out Ethan's war-hammer, which he kept, and crashed the wooden double doors with it.

First there was a small hole, and then a medium sized hole, and then a huge hole. But finally, Trent made a human sized hole, and barged into the obsidian tower with the rest of the ProDyno team.